DATE DUE

DEC 13 '88	OCT. 28 1994
MAY 1 1989	
NOV 1 1 1989	
MAR 0 3 1990	
AUG 0 2 1990	
SEP 1 2 1990	
NOV 2 6 1990	
APR 6 1992	
AUG 1 4 1992	
JUN. 28 1993	
AUG. 3 1993	

Horses
of Dreamland

Horses
of Dreamland

Lois Duncan

Illustrated by Donna Diamond

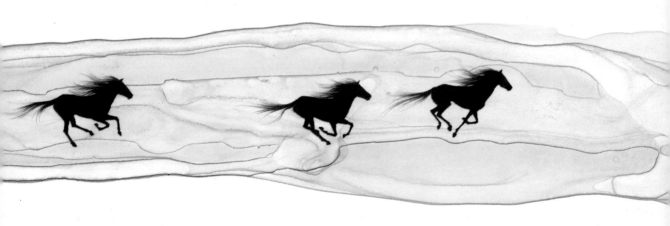

Little, Brown and Company

Boston   *Toronto*

TEXT COPYRIGHT © 1985 BY LOIS DUNCAN

ILLUSTRATIONS COPYRIGHT © 1985 BY DONNA DIAMOND

Second Printing

Library of Congress Cataloging in Publication Data

Duncan, Lois, 1934–
   Horses of dreamland.

   Summary: A child dreams of flying away through the
night with a herd of fantasy horses that subdue a pack
of nightmare wolves before continuing their journey
across earth and heaven.
   1. Children's stories, American.   [1. Stories in
rhyme.   2. Dreams — Fiction.   3. Horses — Fiction]
I. Diamond, Donna, ill.   II. Title.
PZ8.3.D9158Ho   1985   [E]   84-21759
ISBN 0-316-19554-5 (lib. bdg.)

*Published simultaneously in Canada
by Little, Brown & Company (Canada) Limited*

PRINTED IN JAPAN

For my niece,
Ashley Duncan Steinmetz
— *L. D.*

For Rusty
— *D. D.*

A child who dreams of horses

Flies fast and far at night

And travels miles of moon-trail

Before the sky grows bright.

She climbs the peaks of mountains

And struggles through the haze

Until she finds the canyon

Where dreamland horses graze.

The horses hear her summons

And race to heed the call.

They speed across the valley:

They leap the canyon wall.

Their manes are twined with flowers;

Their breath is sweet as hay.

A child can hear their hoofbeats

From many miles away.

A child who dreams of horses

Rides far on starlit trails.

Her hair streams out behind her

With flying manes and tails.

She travels over deserts,
And hillsides, thick with trees,
The twinkling lights of cities,
The churning, white-frothed seas.

The horses mount the heavens;

The world drops far below.

The clouds roll out before them

Like endless drifts of snow.

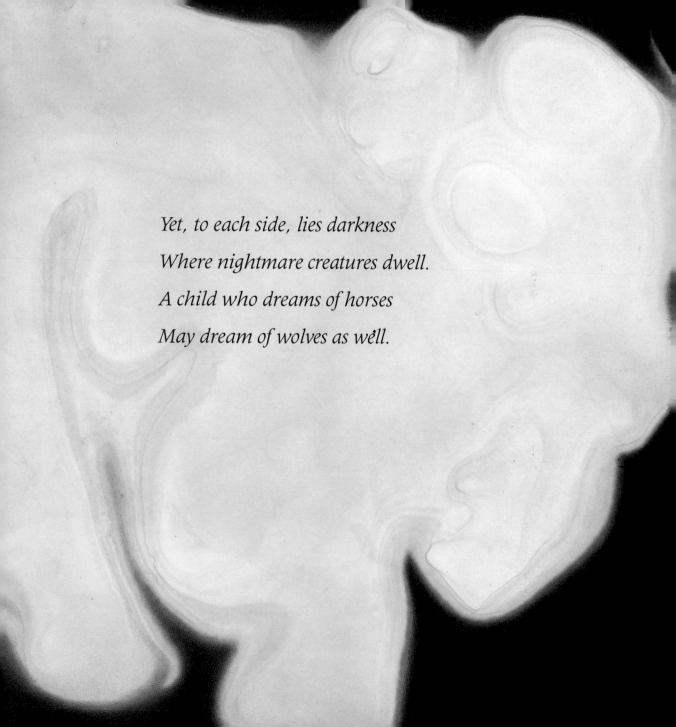

Yet, to each side, lies darkness

Where nightmare creatures dwell.

A child who dreams of horses

May dream of wolves as well.

Like stealthy, red-eyed shadows

They glide into her sleep.

They crouch behind the cloud banks

And brace themselves — and leap.

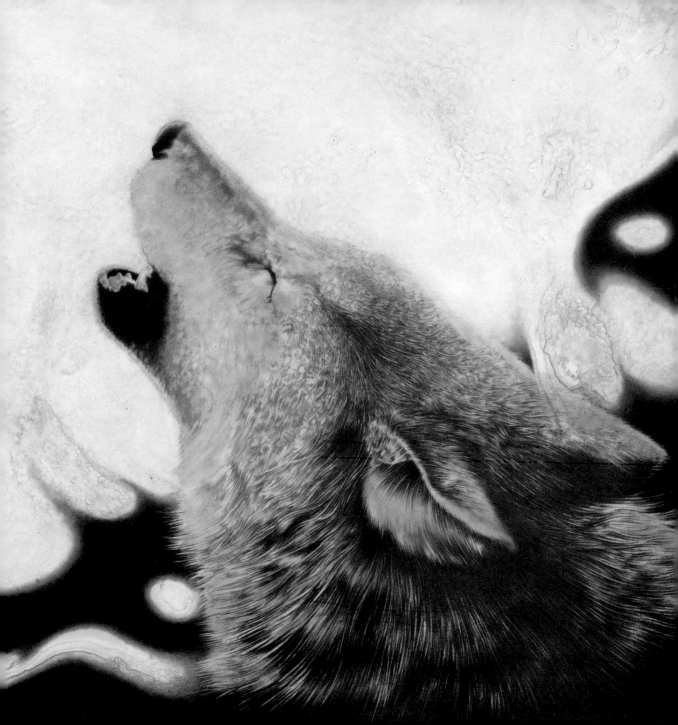

The horses, wild with terror,

Throw back their heads and scream.

The child cries, "Things of evil —

I bid thee — leave my dream!"

Her voice dispels the nightmare.

The savage, snarling wolves

Are trampled into dustmotes

Beneath a thousand hooves.

The horses gallop onward
Toward lands that bear no name,
Until the far horizon
Becomes a streak of flame.

When floods of golden sunlight

Replace the crimson dawn

The child who dreams of horses

Awakes to find them gone.

When she sits down to breakfast

The horses of her dreams

Lie down in misty meadows

Or doze by quiet streams.

Then, as their eyes grow heavy
And close against the light,
They dream of all the children
Who come to them at night.